A Friend for
DRAGON

Read more DRAGON books!

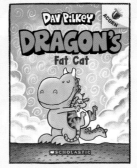

A Friend for
DRAGON

DAV PILKEY

ACORN™
SCHOLASTIC

Published in the UK by Scholastic Children's Books, 2020
Euston House, 24 Eversholt Street, London, NW1 1DB, UK

A division of Scholastic Limited.
London – New York – Toronto – Sydney – Auckland
Mexico City – New Delhi – Hong Kong
SCHOLASTIC and associated logos are trademarks and/or
registered trademarks of Scholastic Inc.
First published in the US by Orchard Books, 1991
This edition first published in the US by Scholastic Inc, 2019
Text and illustration© Dav Pilkey, 1991, 2019

The right of Dav Pilkey to be identified as the author and illustrator of this work has been
asserted by him under the Copyright, Designs and Patents Act 1988.

ISBN 978 0702 30164 3

A CIP catalogue record for this book is available from the British Library.

All rights reserved.

This book is sold subject to the condition that it shall not,
by way of trade or otherwise, be lent, hired out or otherwise circulated in
any form of binding or cover other than that in which it is published. No
part of this publication may be reproduced, stored in a retrieval system,
or transmitted in any form or by any means (electronic, mechanical,
photocopying, recording or otherwise) without prior
written permission of Scholastic Limited.
Printed by CPI Group (UK) Ltd, Croydon, CR0 4YY
Papers used by Scholastic Children's Books are made
from wood grown in sustainable forests.
1 3 5 7 9 10 8 6 4 2

This is a work of fiction. Names, characters, places, incidents
and dialogues are products of the author's imagination or are used
fictitiously. Any resemblance to actual people, living or dead,
events or locales is entirely coincidental.
www.scholastic.co.uk

Contents

1
A Friend for Dragon

There once was a blue dragon
who lived in a little house
all by himself.
Sometimes Dragon got lonely.

"I wish I had a friend," said Dragon.
So he went out into the world
to look for a friend.

Dragon went to the woods
and met a small black squirrel.

"Will you be my friend?"
said Dragon.

"No," said the squirrel.
"I'm too busy."

Dragon went to the riverbank
and met a fat grey hippo.

"Will you be my friend?"
said Dragon.

"No," said the hippo.
"I'm too tired."

Dragon went to the pond
and met a slick green crocodile.

"Will you be my friend?"
said Dragon.

"No," said the crocodile.
"I'm too grouchy."

So Dragon sat down under a tree,
still wishing for a friend.

Suddenly, an apple fell out
of the tree and hit Dragon
on the head.

Just then, a little green snake
slithered by.
The snake wanted to
play a joke on Dragon.
So it hid behind a rock
and called out, "Hi, Dragon."

Dragon looked all around,
but he didn't see anyone.
"Who said that?" cried Dragon.

"I did," said the snake.

Dragon looked all around again,
but he still didn't see anyone.

"Where are you?" said Dragon.

"I'm right here in your hand," said the snake.

Dragon looked at the apple in his hand and scratched his big head.

"I did not know apples
could talk," said Dragon.

"Oh, but we can,"
said the snake in the grass.

"Would you like to be my friend?"
Dragon asked the apple.

"Oh, yes," laughed the snake.

"At last," said Dragon.
"A friend."

2
Friends at Home

Dragon took the apple home
and built a warm, cosy fire.

He told spooky stories to the apple.
He told funny jokes to the apple.
Dragon talked all day long
and into the night.

"You are a good listener,"
said Dragon.
"Good friends are always
good listeners."

Dragon fixed a midnight snack.
He mixed cookies, orange juice
and ketchup all together in a big bowl.

Dragon scooped some of the food
on to his plate.
Then he scooped some food onto the
apple's plate.

"Just say 'When,'" said Dragon.
The apple did not say "When."

So Dragon scooped some more food
on to the apple's plate.

"Just say 'When,'" Dragon said.
The apple still did not say "When."

17

So Dragon scooped the rest of the food on to the apple's plate.

"I am glad that we both like to eat so much," said Dragon. "Good friends should always have a lot in common."

Dragon ate up all of his food.
The apple did not eat any food at all.

Dragon was still hungry.
He looked at the apple's plate
and drooled.

"Do you mind if I eat some
of your food?" asked Dragon.

The apple did not seem to mind.

So Dragon ate up all of the apple's
food too.

"You are a good friend," said Dragon.
"Good friends always share."

3
The New Day

The next morning, Dragon awoke
with the sun.

"Good morning, Apple," said Dragon.
The apple did not answer.

So Dragon went out to the kitchen
and made breakfast.

When he was finished eating,
he tried to wake the apple up again.

"Good morning, Apple," he cried.
The apple still did not answer.

So Dragon went outside
for a walk along the riverbank.

When he came back,
he tried to wake the apple up again.

"GOOD MORNING, APPLE!" he screamed.
The apple still did not answer.

Dragon was very worried.
He called the doctor.

"My apple won't talk to me,"
said Dragon.

"Maybe it's a crab apple,"
said the doctor.

"No," said Dragon.
"I think it is sick."

So Dragon took the apple
to the doctor's office.
They sat down next to a big walrus.

"What's the matter with you?"
asked the walrus.

"It's my apple," said Dragon.
"It won't talk to me."

The walrus stared at the apple
and drooled.

Dragon needed a drink of water.
"Will you watch my apple for me?"
Dragon asked the walrus.

"Sure," said the walrus,
licking her lips.

When Dragon came back,
the apple had changed.
It was not round any more.
It was not shiny any more.
It was not red any more.
Now it was wet and skinny and white.

"What happened to you?" cried Dragon. "Are you all right?"

The little white thing did not answer.

Dragon wrapped his friend
in a piece of paper
and carried it home.

"Don't worry," said Dragon.
"Everything will be OK."

When Dragon got home,
the little white thing had turned all
mushy and brown.

"Are you hurt?" asked Dragon.
The mushy brown thing did not answer.

"Are you sick?" asked Dragon.
But there was no answer.

"Are you dead?" asked Dragon.
Still, there was no answer.

Dragon scratched his big head
and started to cry.

4
Goodbye

The next morning,
Dragon went out into his garden
and dug a hole.

He put his friend into the hole
and covered it over with dirt.

Dragon made a sign.
On the sign, he wrote the word
"Friend."

45

Dragon was very sad.
He cried every day.
He did not want to eat.
He could not get to sleep.
Dragon did not leave his house
for a long, long time.

But after a while,
Dragon stopped being so sad.
He cried less and less.
He began to eat and sleep better.

Still, he was very lonely.

48

5
Summertime

One day, many months later,
Dragon walked out into his garden.
He was still feeling lonely.
Dragon sat down under the big tree
growing in his yard.
He wished for a friend.

Suddenly, something fell
out of the tree and hit Dragon
on the head.

It was an apple.

Then Dragon looked up, and smiled.

About the Author

Dav Pilkey is the creator of the bestselling Dog Man and Captain Underpants series. He has written and illustrated many other books for young readers, including the Dumb Bunnies series, *The Hallo-Wiener*, *Dog Breath*, and *The Paperboy*, which is a Caldecott Honour book. Dav lives in the Pacific Northwest with his wife.

YOU CAN DRAW DRAGON!

 Draw a backward letter "C."

 Draw the top of Dragon's head and the back of his neck.

 Put a smile on his face.

 Add his eyes and nose.

5 Add horns on top of his head.

6 Draw Dragon's arm. He's waving at you!

7 Add his tummy and other arm.

8 Draw his tail.

9 Add one foot.

10 Add the other foot.

11 Draw spikes down his back and on his tail.

12 Colour in your drawing!

YOU CAN DRAW APPLE!

1 Draw a circle that has a dip on the top.

2 Draw a line coming out of the dip. It's the stem!

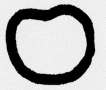

3 Add a leaf to the stem.

4 Colour in your drawing!

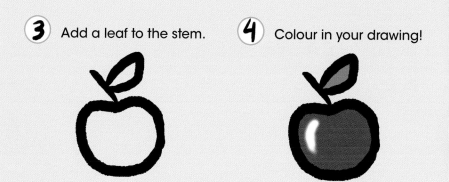

WHAT'S YOUR STORY?

Dragon and his new friend have fun together.
Imagine **you** and Dragon are friends.
What would you do for fun?
What snack would you make?
Write and draw your story!

BONUS!

Try making your story just like Dav –
with watercolours! Did you know that
Dav taught himself how to watercolour
when he was making this book? He went
to the supermarket, bought a children's watercolour
set, and used it to paint all the Dragon books.

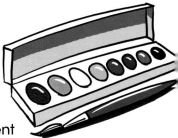